# To Abide in
# His Shadow

# To Abide in His Shadow

Tyler Brooks

Rev. date: 04/25/2016

**To order additional copies of this book, contact:**
Xlibris
1-888-795-4274
www.Xlibris.com
Orders@Xlibris.com
738524

Although there exists a perpetual noise in New York City, the constant motion of a multitude of urban dwellers, the busy lives of millions, swinging, swaying, vibrating separately and as one, encircling one another, the night is dead. The voices of the millions are simply a placeholder for the silence which is imposed upon the world's capital, when *he* is about his business. When he speaks, will not the entire world drop its work and pause, out of fear, and awe, out of terrified respect? His word is more important, carries more authority than the revered leaders of the land, whether he speaks to the mass or to himself in the mirror before bed.

Some say he was born from the secrets of the city. Some believe that he has huge armies at his command. There are a few who would swear before God that they see him in mirrors, hiding in shadows, following everywhere they go. Everyone knows he is to be feared. The rumors may be speculation; the fact is that there isn't a politician in office in the city, not a bootlegger on the streets, not a businessman on Wall Street who isn't under his thumb.

An adverse situation can break a man, can crush a mediocre man, can crumple an ordinary man. But the same scenario can expose an extraordinary man, can pull a man with potential to his destined greatness. He was a known man, a respected and feared man prior to Prohibition, but this new law had introduced him to a level of prestige known only to a select few. In a few short years, the once-small-time gangster pulled himself from the shadows of the city, and by the manipulation of an unfortunate situation, the dark ambition, quiet cruelty, and charismatic evil of Ricky Malone was placed on the throne of New York City. By the year 1929, his was a power paralleled by none. The imposition of his will and his orchestration of the lives of the people in his town are exacted by way of low whispers through a telephone, in an abandoned warehouse on the Hudson guarded as if it were a palace; one of his many hideouts. "No. No possible way. To steal money from me is one thing, but to steal from him…no. *È incredibile.* I tell you, this Irish mob is getting totally outta control. Believe you me, if it was a different situation, I was a few years younger, I'd wish every one of 'em sweet dreams at the bottom of the river…" Malone pulls an infant cloud out of the butt of his Cuban cigar, releases it back into the sky, places the lit cigar into the ashtray, and continues to think about the issue placed before him.

"Perhaps it was my mistake. I was ignorant for placing the money directly into their hands." He anxiously spins the cylinder of his revolver with his free hand as he contemplates. He stands up, placing the gun on the desk and his hand on his forehead. Pacing back and forth, he pulls the wire of the telephone taut and retracts it multiple times. There is no voice on the other end of the line. Sitting back down, Malone says, "If you come across Scraps, tell him to find me," and promptly hangs up the phone. He leans back in the chair and closes his eyes, letting out a sigh. He sits here for several minutes, breathing extremely heavily. Ricky Malone, the most feared man in all the boroughs, notorious along the entire East Coast, has not been this burdened in decades. Not since he had climbed the ranks of the New York underworld. Malone has not had a serious care since he amassed his huge wealth. Even as a six-year-old boy, a new immigrant from Naples, a poor boy who had nothing but the clothes on his back, Malone did not worry to the extent to which he worries now. Nearly sixty years of life have not taught him to cope with such hardship. He glances at the shining pistol on his desk. Picking it up, he very slowly raises the muzzle to the roof of his mouth. The metal is cold on his lips and his tongue. Malone hears the click as he ever so slowly pulls back the hammer of the gun. His finger touches the trigger for just a moment, and before he knows it, the gun is back on the desk with a thud. Adrenaline tears through his body. It is not the first time Malone has entertained the horrid idea. He wipes drops of sweat from his forehead, and unloads the pistol before shoving it into his coat pocket. Throwing the fedora on his head, he briskly walks out of the warehouse, to where his men and his car are awaiting him. "Let's get outta here." The men follow and load into the car, and they disappear into the night.

*    *    *

It is true throughout all the world, and all the more painfully true in the slums of Brooklyn, that bad things happen to good people. Good, honest people, hardworking New Yorkers toil their entire lives and are screwed over nonetheless, every day of the week. This is especially true for a particular skinny eighteen-year-old. To some, he may just be the poor young Knickerbocker who sweeps up cut hair at the barbershop, but his tale is much more melancholy.

The fatherless child who grew up in a three hundred square-foot apartment in Brooklyn with his mother, a waitress at a diner not too far from home, he's the brightest student in the neighborhood. Some say he might be the brightest in all the boroughs, maybe the world. Throughout his life he's always had his nose pressed up against the interior of the spine of a book, studying hard, or reading for pleasure. His painstaking efforts had finally paid off – or so he thought. His work had earned him a spot at Harvard University. He'd be the first in his family to attend college.

He had it all worked out – he'd made sure he earned straight A's from the first grade to the twelfth, to ensure that he would get into college. That was the hard part, and hard it was indeed. But he made it through. Now how would a poor Brooklyn boy ever be able to afford university, you may ask. This was the easy part. His whole life, he'd been told there was a small fortune awaiting him in the bank, ripening for his eighteenth birthday. The sum of $5,000 would pay for his college education, and then law school, after which he'd become a lawyer, and even later a politician, maybe even mayor of New York. He'd stick up for the little guys, like himself, and defend justice. He'd be perhaps the last clean man in power, one who couldn't be bought for a cheap sum.

He never knew where the money had come from – perhaps his mother did, but she would never tell. He always assumed it was from his father, attempting to win his son's admiration with a purchase by cold cash rather than a demonstration of parenthood. This was the one bribe that he could not refuse.

However, there is a reason that he'd cried himself to sleep every night since his eighteenth birthday. The eager boy who had run to the bank to cash in was let down. His money was gone. It was like it had never been there. "Sorry, kid," the bank teller had said with a slight grin. Those two words played over and over in his head without end.

For weeks, he wondered "Why? How?"

Then he remembered, it was a mafia bank. Everyone knew. The loss of his fortune was just another horrible example of the corruption of the fat cats in his city, men in power who'd been bought off by rich gangsters. This time they stole his fortune, they stole his education, they stole his hope, they stole his future. The very people that he would have gone to school to stop had killed any hope of that before he even had a chance. They'd nipped him in the bud. Perhaps it was some cruel, dark fate; perhaps the gangsters were meant to be on top forever, and good was never supposed to be allowed a chance.

So instead of going to a prestigious university, becoming an educated man of power who vowed himself incorruptible, instead of being empowered to put down men the likes of which had just robbed him, it is more long hours at the barbershop.

*Just keep your head down and sweep, boy. Sweep, sweep, sweep.*

Woe, thy name is Bobby Falcone.

\*     \*     \*

"Scraps is here to see you," one of Malone's men whispers into his ear.

"Let him in," Malone forms the words around the fat butt of an unlit cigar. He is alone for a moment as his henchman goes to fetch the informant who has arrived to speak with him at his home. It is nearly midnight. The den in Malone's mansion is dark other than a small reading lamp on the large mahogany desk behind which he lounges in a chair, and his large roaring fireplace.

After a few moments, the door creaks open once more, and a short, stumpy, dirty looking man dressed in rags with a pitiful five o'clock shadow walks in.

"Jesus, Scraps. Took you long enough to make your way up."

The man looks around, in frightened awe of the beautiful home in which he currently stands, though it is hardly his first visit.

"My apologies, sir," he rasps. "It was hard for me to make my way all the way out here. What can I help you with?" He never looks Malone directly in the eye.

Malone looks at the man called Scraps for a few moments. Of all the ears Malone has on the streets of the Big Apple, Scraps is the most reliable. It is also greatly to Malone's convenience that he walks the streets of Brooklyn. He'd helped Malone out on numerous occasions. Malone paid him next to nothing. Knowing he was a vicious alcoholic before Prohibition was enacted, Malone paid Scraps just enough to buy a bottle of whiskey or two underground. A few times, he had simply paid him in whiskey. Men like Scraps would do anything for a drink.

Malone thinks about Scraps' desperation for the burn of alcohol down his throat, then thinks of his own desperation for his current situation to be resolved. However, he cannot let it show. Even to a low-life like Scraps, Malone must appear a king. He cannot give the slightest inkling of fear of any magnitude.

"I got a special job for you today, Scraps."

"What you got for me in return?" Scraps says without hesitation, eyes wide, peering behind Malone's desk.

"What do I got?" Malone says in a hushed voice, with a chuckle.

Reaching to the floor underneath his desk, Malone draws an unopened bottle of Jim Beam. Seeing the look of uncontrollable desire on Scraps' face, Malone flashes his devilish smile and says, "Like that, huh?"

"What do you wanna know? Anything, sir," Scraps says, never taking his eyes off of the bottle in Malone's grasp.

Malone places the bottle back on the floor and loudly snaps his fingers, to gain Scraps' full, undivided attention.

"It's not information I want. I need you to send someone to me."

"Send you someone…Who?" Scraps says, a dazed, confused look on his face.

"There's a boy I need to talk to. A boy who lives not far from you," Malone says, all his effort in keeping the apprehension out of his voice.

"What boy?" Scraps says anxiously.

"I need to have a few words with a boy by the name of Roberto Falcone."

Scraps looks down for a moment. "Roberto Falc… Oh Bobby? The kid who works down at the barbershop? Yeah, him and his mother live just…" Scraps sees the terrifying look of impatient anger on Malone's face, and stops.

"So, what do you want with him?"

"That, Scraps, is my business. Stick to yours. If you want so much as a drop of this, I'll see the boy by the end of this week. If you cannot get him to see me, I will find someone who will."

The look on Scraps' face at the thought of not getting Malone's whiskey is unmitigated dread. "No sir! I'll get him to come see you. I'll make sure he understands, Ricky Malone wants him."

"No, what are you an idiot?" Malone spits at the bum.

"Sir…?"

"The boy isn't involved in any of our kinda business, I've never spoken to him. Why would I want to see him? Get him here without mentioning that I want him. Talk to the boy. Make him want to come here."

Scraps looks at Malone, baffled beyond what he can say. His mouth moves, without sound, as he tries to find the words to say to the kingpin who sits before him.

"If you aren't up for the job…" Malone says quietly, raising the bottle of whiskey back up, rotating it in his hands.

"No!" Scraps shouts, staring at the bottle again, nearly in tears. "I can do it." He takes a deep breath. "I'll send the boy your way."

Malone smirks, and says "Good. Now get outta my sight."

Scraps is gone, and immediately the King-like façade falls from Malone's being. He lights his cigar, takes a long puff and blows a huge cloud of smoke into the air around his head. He breathes very heavily, and buries his face in his hand.

*How will I look the boy in the eye?*

Malone has never feared another man in his entire life, why is he so petrified about being in the same room as an eighteen-year-old boy?

However, it is not just meeting the boy which frightens Malone. He reflects on his life, on his career, on the empire he's built. More than anything, he thinks of the wrong he has done, the blood he has spilt. Never has it bothered him until now. After almost sixty years, has Malone finally grown a conscience? Why is he so burdened?

He knows what must be done.

There are plenty of variables, but deep down, Ricky Malone knows the events which are about to unfold, and he is scared to death. For the first time in all his life, the King of New York is paralyzed by fear.

\*　　\*　　\*

Walking home from a long tedious day of work, the scent of alcohol and hair products hanging in his nose and still hearing the chatter of the dirty old men who have themselves groomed in the barbershop where he works echoing in his mind, Bobby Falcone's deepest desire is to see his bed and escape to sleep. It's about a four-block walk from his workplace to his home. Some people would be nervous walking through the shanty neighborhoods of Brooklyn at night, but for Bobby, it's as normal as breathing.

He walks at a fast pace, head down, trying to get home as fast as possible. His speed-walk is nearly a jog. He hardly has to look where he steps – his feet know the way home after walking the route what feels to Bobby like millions of times.

*Step, step, step, step, step, step, step, ste-*

Bobby Falcone accidentally walks into a man walking in the opposite direction on the sidewalk. He is immediately assaulted with the stench of tobacco and the muck of the streets as he collides with this man. As Bobby looks to the man's face to apologize, he is surprised to see a familiar face. He is considerably shorter than Bobby, and has a huge belly. His clothes look as though they haven't been changed or washed for weeks, and he has a tatty winter hat on over his scraggly hair, although it is not cold out.

"Well if it ain't young Bobby Falcone!" the old man rasps with a smile.

"How you doing, Scraps," Bobby replies quietly, looking over the man's shoulder. He does not want to stop to talk. Scraps is a bum in his neighborhood who knows nearly everyone by name, and talks to everyone who passes him by. He's a genial old man, but it's rumored that he's involved with unsavory characters – this is not surprising to many, being that he can often be seen with alcoholic beverages in his hand in broad daylight, without a care whether he is caught with contraband materials.

"Bobby Falcone, the smartest boy in the city!" Scraps smiles for a few moments, but the smile fades to a look of troubled disappointment. He says in a more quieted voice, "Listen, I heard about your situation with those so-and-so's down at the bank."

Bobby's mood plummets to an even lower point than where it had already been. He's already had to explain to numerous people – at work, at school, family members, folks from the neighborhood – why he wouldn't be attending university. If he has to hear "How could it just disappear!" or "Bobby Falcone won't be attending college?" or "You have no more money saved up at all?" one more time, he feels he would explode.

"Such a shame," Scraps continues, "but who would leave you money in that bank anyway? Every mook in Brooklyn knows that Gallagher and the Irish gangsters have been running that joint for years."

"I don't know," Bobby says, agitated. "I'm guessing my pop was rich or somethin', left me the money before he split. I guess he wasn't in the know about who ran the bank. But that's it, I suppose. No money, no college, no nothin'. Come fall, I'll be right here in Brooklyn with you."

Scraps looks down, with the same hurt look of being let down that everyone wore when Bobby told them about his money being stolen. He looks back up at Bobby and says, "You know, I always thought that if anyone could make it out of this neighborhood, if anyone could make a name for himself and become more than a bootlegger, or a bum like me, it'd be you. Everyone did. Bobby Falcone, the one good thing to come out of this neighborhood. Brooklyn's own jewel." His voice trails off.

Bobby's eyes are watering, and he feels he is about to burst into tears. He has heard this speech over and over and over, and just wants to leave. It is not easy knowing that everyone feels let down by him not going to college. Being raised in an area where everyone is under the control of gangsters and crime lords, where everyone is too poor to ever leave the neighborhood they grew up in, where your neighbors and best friends are looked at as scum by people who live in other boroughs, even though they are a part of the same city, everyone needs a little hope. Until quite recently, that was Bobby. No one from his neighborhood has ever been intrepid enough to stand up and make a difference. There's never been anyone in power in the city with a heart like his, with the intention of running the city honestly, refusing any kind of buyoff by the gangsters. Everyone was waiting for Bobby. Now, it seems, all their hopes have been dashed.

Suddenly, Scraps looks up at Bobby. His eyes widened and his brows raised, he looks east and west and says, "Bobby, I live on these streets. I've seen a lot and I know a lot of people. Everyone in this neighborhood is riding on you." He pauses for a moment and Bobby stares at him, not sure where he is going.

"I think I know someone who can help you."

Immediately, Bobby's interest is peaked. He has been so miserable these past weeks, he is desperate to believe that there is any hope of attending college, any hope at all.

Scraps scratches his head and says, "He's uh, he's a businessman. Takes care of these sorts of things. He's very good at what he does. He's helped out a lot of people in your situation. Seen it myself."

"So what is he, like a banker?" Bobby begins to get excited, his body tensing, as he hangs on to every word Scraps says.

"He handles a lot of finances, lots of money and business transactions. Like I said, he's more of a businessman than a banker. But he's got no affiliation with Gallagher or those Irish scum who stole your money at that gangster bank, I can tell you that for sure," Scraps waves his hand and shakes his head as he says this, conveying his confidence in the man he is describing.

"Well, where can I find him?" Bobby asks with impatient arousal.

"I don't know everything about this fella, but I do know where he works from," Scraps replies.

"Tell me, please! Ah, jeez, Scraps, if this guy can help me…"

"Now he will charge you, but I figure five grand? I don't think he'd ask for more than ten percent. Fifteen tops."

"Scraps, where do I go to find him?" Bobby says, growing more irritated, losing the excitement attached to his impatience.

"Alright, alright, hold your horses," Scraps says, "Give me something to write with."

Bobby searches his person, and to his stark relief, he has a pencil in his left pocket. He hands it to Scraps after finding it.

Scraps looks around for something to write on, but cannot find anything. After a moment he says "Ah crap," to himself and pulls on Bobby's hand. He then proceeds to crudely and barely visibly write an address on the inside of Bobby's forearm. Bobby has a hard time making it out, but he can. The address is unfamiliar to Bobby. All he knows is that it's in Brooklyn.

"Tomorrow night," Scraps says abruptly. "Meet him here around nine o'clock."

"Nine?" Bobby asks, "Kinda late for a businessman. Don't you think I oughtta go earli-"

"No!" Scraps cuts him off.

Bobby is surprised by this, wondering why Scraps interrupted him and suddenly seems so hostile.

Scraps then gives a small smile and says "He's just a very busy man. Lots of other affairs to take care of, understand?"

"Oh," Bobby says quietly. "Uh, okay. So tomorrow night at nine. Do I need to make an appointment?"

"No," Scraps says, shaking his head. "He uh, he's very open to walk-ins. Says he likes to keep an open-door policy."

Bobby nods his head, staring at the address written on his arm, a bit skeptical, but so desperate for anyone to help him that he does not dare seem cynical or question the man Scraps has just directed him to.

"Alright, Scraps, well thanks a lot. I appreciate it. I owe you one," Bobby gives Scraps a heavy pat on the shoulder, then turns to continue walking home. After taking a few steps, he calls back, "Hey, Scraps! What's this guy's name?" However, turning around after he loudly asks his question, Bobby finds that Scraps has crossed the street and is already about a half a block away, walking in the opposite direction. He must have run to have gotten there so quickly. Bobby wonders for a moment why Scraps left so quickly, but soon assumes that Scraps had simply forgotten to mention the man's name, and he disregards it. He continues his walk home, for the first time in weeks, with a smile on his face. All he has been searching for is the slightest inkling that his entire future wasn't snatched out from under him, and this mystery man who he plans to meet tomorrow provides just that.

\*    \*    \*

The black curtain of night has fallen on the city as the mad, old man stumbles about his home. What would the people of New York think? What would the terrified commoners of the city feel, to see their almighty tyrant as he is now, a drunken fool who can hardly make the journey from his den to his bedroom. He falls over his furniture, colliding with his walls, tripping over his own feet. It's as though Ricky Malone is trying to walk to his room with his house being rotated counterclockwise.

There is no reason for Malone to continue to pretend he is fearless, that he is all-powerful, that he is untouchable. There is no reason for him to be anything but the raw, shameful, terrified man, a shell of his former self, when he is alone in his house with his thoughts – and his whiskey. In the solitude of his home, he can afford to dwell on his fear, to indulge in the immense burden which crushes his soul, the guilt and shame of a life of wrong. With every bang of his feet against a piece of furniture, Malone hears the bang of his pistol, aimed squarely between his victim's eyes. With every thud Malone makes as his body hits a wall, he hears the bodies of his victims hitting the ground. With every grunt he makes as he painstakingly tries to reach his bed, he hears the screams of all the people over the years who have cried in terror at the mention of his name.

He's never felt guilty before. Ricky Malone had done everything necessary to build his empire without remorse. However, recently, there have been increasingly more and more nights like this one. For some reason, the silence of his huge estate has been scolding him recently, reminding him of the grave wrongs he's committed. On these nights, the burn of the whiskey is the only thing that drowns out Malone's own conscience. But since he heard of the boy Falcone's money being stolen, his conscience has been screaming louder than ever. Tonight, the whiskey does not burn hot enough.

*The boy is my last hope,* he thinks, crawling up his stairs.

*The boy will fix everything.*

He finally reaches the top, and continues to crawl to protect himself from falling and injuring himself.

Gallagher's theft of Falcone's money infuriated Malone further than anything up until this point. The boy needed the money. Malone *needed* the boy to have that money.

"That dirty Irish...", Malone thinks. "That...dirty Irish scum!" he slurs loudly to himself.

Braden Gallagher may have been considered a major kingpin, were he not in New York. In Malone's city, he's small potatoes. Just another gangster. Malone has never feared him, but in the last few years, he's become a greater and greater pain in Malone's neck. Malone didn't give him too much attention, but stealing the boy's money was the last straw. He had to be set straight.

What will you do, murder him in cold blood?

Malone shakes. He doesn't want to kill anymore. He's participated enough in that dirty business.

The boy will fix everything.

But will it? Will helping the boy be enough to make up for the wrong he has done?

"What on earth's the matter with you?"

Who said that? Malone turns around, and faces the mirror on his wall. The reflection in the mirror is a much different Malone. He is years younger. Tall. Proud. Dressed in an all black suit and overcoat, with a black fedora on his head, he is the image of the terrifying mafia king known to the people of New York. He frightens even the old drunken man who is spread out on the floor before him.

"Are you going soft?" He sneers. "Sitting here, crying like a baby. Get up off your butt and ice that Irish scum!"

"No, I can't," Malone says, looking longingly at the mirror. "I can't murd-"

"You can't murder? You have the audacity to say that after all these years of giving the angel of death himself a run for his money." The Malone in the mirror chuckles. "You're pitiful."

It is silent for a moment.

"I'm not pitiful," he says quietly, after what seems like a lifetime. "I just don't want to be a cheap assassin. I just want to help the boy."

"That's not what you've been saying all these years. That's not what you said every single time you've been double-crossed, lied to, or screwed out of money. But now, after all these decades, when you're on top of the world, you've suddenly had a change of heart? Pick up your pistol and smoke that Irish pig. Snap out of it! This ain't your first rodeo!"

"Look. The truth is-"

"Don't you know that I am the truth?"

Malone is silent for a moment.

"Would you be sitting here in this king's mansion, sipping that expensive whiskey if it weren't for me? I brought you to where you are today. I made us king of the world. It's all because of me."

"No," Malone says.

"Kill him."

"No," he says a bit louder.

"Ice that dirty Irish scum!"

"NO!" Malone shouts, taking off a shoe and throwing it at the mirror. He has had enough. As the mirror shatters with a loud crash, the other Malone fades, his voice quieting until it is nonexistent.

Ricky makes it to his bed, finally. As he rests his head on his pillow and begins to drift away, he knows exactly what he is to do.

Although it pains him to admit, deep down he feels that the Malone in the mirror was not completely wrong.

There are two things that Ricky Malone prides himself on: he is absolutely lethal with a handgun, from nearly any distance, and he has an uncanny ability to create a plan and execute it to perfection, no matter how many people the plan involves, no matter the variables. Ricky Malone orchestrates the affairs of the Big Apple's underworld as well as many affairs of the known world.

He needs to return Bobby Falcone's money to him, he needs to be rid of Braden Gallagher once and for all, and perhaps above all, he needs to be freed of the horrible shadow of his past, all the sins he has committed, all the lives he has destroyed.

Lying in his bed, even falling into an intoxicated stupor, Ricky Malone knows exactly what he is to do.

*     *     *

Today has been the longest day of Bobby Falcone's life. As he sits in the back of the tatty taxicab, he is nervous, and excited, and a bit scared. His emotions have been tossed all over the room. From having huge aspirations of attending university and looking forward to a bright future, to having that dream suddenly stripped from him, to one day being given a small hope that it may be returned to him, Bobby feels emotionally like a bone being fought over by two Dobermans.

He's been in the cab for about a half hour, unsure of where exactly he is headed. When he gave the address to the driver at the start of the trip, the driver said, "Why on earth would you wanna go there?" Bobby explained that he would be meeting with a businessman to discuss an issue, to which the driver gave a look of understanding, and proceeded to drive without another word.

After a half hour of sitting in the back of a cab, his leg shaking, nervously analyzing every detail of every building they passed, Bobby is slightly startled by the driver saying, "Alright, kid." Bobby pays the driver, and exits the cab.

He is discomforted by what he sees.

Bobby stands in front of a string of uninhabited office buildings on the edge of town. He's seen this area before in passing, but never thought anything of it. He wonders if Scraps gave him the wrong address.

He proceeds slowly, unsure if he should continue at all. He had memorized the address that Scraps gave him. The number of the building was 72. He walks through the area, not hearing a sound. There is not a soul in sight. He passes the buildings 68, 69, 70, 71. He looks back, seeing that the cab is long gone. Here in the dark of night in the abandoned area, Bobby feels like the last man on earth. He has the stark feeling that he should not be here, but cannot turn back. This may be his only opportunity to meet with this man.

After what feels like ages, he arrives at number 72.

He stands before the door, hesitant to go in. He was once excited to meet this man, but now a deep fear is crawling up inside him like a cockroach scaling the drain of a bathroom sink.

He places his hand on the doorknob and holds it there for a moment. Bobby takes a deep breath, turns the knob, and pushes it open.

As soon as he enters he sees three men sitting around a table. They are all about in their thirties, dressed formally in shirt and tie. Two of them have on black suit jackets, but one of them has his white shirt and suspenders exposed. This is the man who jumps up when Bobby enters. He is shorter than Bobby, and extremely thin. He has very sharp facial features, eyes which pop out of his skull, and shiny pitch-black hair which is greased back. The most unsettling thing about this man, though, is the deep scar which runs from the outer corner of his right eye nearly to his chin.

"Hey!" he says in a nasal, abrasive voice. "You're in the wrong place, kid." Bobby is scared, as the man continues to get closer and closer to him as he speaks.

"No," Bobby says like a nervous child, "I-I'm here to talk to a businessman, about some money in my bank account."

"Businessman?" the man says. "Giuseppe, you hear this guy? Businessman." He begins to laugh.

The man Giuseppe, who is quite large and seated, does not laugh along.

"Wait a minute, Bones," he begins in a deep and commanding voice. "Boss said he was meeting with some kid tonight. What's your name, kid?"

"Bobby Falcone," he says.

The three men look at each other for a moment. After an uncomfortable silence, Giuseppe says, "Right up those stairs." He gestures to a staircase to their left.

"Thanks," Bobby says, and continues to the stairs quickly, eager to be away from those men.

Bones? What kind of people are these? Who on earth did Scraps send him to see?

He walks slowly, hesitantly up the stairs. They creak as he does. The staircase is not well lit, and from what he can see, neither is the upstairs. He can hear a faint voice at the top. When he reaches the top, he sees a long hallway, about fifty feet. There are shut doors on either side of the hall, and one door which hangs ajar at the opposite end from the staircase. This is where the voice is coming from.

Bobby tiptoes as if walking on eggshells down the hall. His heart is attempting to pound its way out of his chest, and his forehead is sweating. The air is hot and he finds it hard to breathe, though he makes his breaths as quiet as he can so as not to disturb the man in the room, although he is about to meet with him anyway.

As he draws closer, he can hear more clearly that the man is speaking Italian.

*"These idiots have taken their last shot at me. I swear. They will regret the day they ever crossed my path. They think they're the first ones to try and hurt me. Do they really think they're safe? Don't they know who I am?"*

Bobby is horrified by what he's hearing. Did Scraps send him to meet with some gangster?

No, that couldn't be the case. Scraps said he was a businessman who helped people out with financial problems. He said he'd seen him help plenty of people before Bobby. But then, exactly what kind of businessman could help someone get money back that was stolen by the Irish mob?

But Scraps said that the man he was sending Bobby to had no connections to the gangsters. Didn't he?

Before he knew it, Bobby had knocked twice on the door. He immediately wished he had waited to do it, but knew it was too late — he couldn't take it back.

*"Hang on. There's someone here. I'll be in touch,"* the voice says. Bobby hears the click of a phone being hung up.

"Who's there?" the same voice says in English, sounding vaguely annoyed.

"It's uh," *What's his name? Oh, God.*

"It's Bobby Falcone," he says quickly.

"Alright, get in," the voice says.

Bobby pushes the door open to see a dark room. It is not lit except for the light that enters through the shuttered window, and a small lamp on a desk on the opposite side of the room. Bobby sees a man sitting behind the desk, leaning back in a chair, but cannot make out his features. He can, however, see the red glow of a lit cigar protruding from the man's mouth, and a half-full glass on the desk.

"Have a seat, Mr. Falcone," he says.

Bobby can hear faint traces of an Italian accent in the man's speech, but not much. Bobby can tell by his voice that he is an older man.

Still more nervous than he has ever been before, Bobby makes his way across the dark room, and finds the seat. He pulls it out, and slowly sits down.

The man takes the cigar out of his mouth with his left hand, and extends the right toward Bobby. Bobby takes his hand and shakes it.

"A pleasure to meet with you this evening, Mr. Falcone," he begins. "The name is Ricky Malone."

Immediately, Bobby's heart falls out of his butt. He draws one sharp breath without thinking, then believes that he may never breathe again.

Ricky Malone is a name muttered around New York in terrified whispers. He is supposed to be the man behind every crooked deal and every shady encounter, the reason there are so many corrupt cops and politicians in the city. It is *his* money which bought all the power in the Big Apple. It is Malone who is said to be the source of all criminal affairs, both the ones that make the newspapers, and the ones no one would ever hear of. Should someone mysteriously turn up missing, one can guess he had something to do with it. His name is used as the explanation for every sketchy occurrence in the city, to the point where some people question whether or not he even truly exists. Perhaps he is just like the boogeyman, a thing of nightmares. But Bobby has always known. The most terrifying thing about Ricky Malone is that he is real. Bobby would've suspected it was *he* who was behind the quiet disappearance of his money, other than the fact that he knows it's Gallagher and the Irish gang who run the bank that his five grand was sitting in.

Scraps didn't just send Bobby to a gangster. He sent Bobby to *the* gangster.

Ricky Malone is the epitome of everything Bobby stands against. He hates organized crime, and now he is sitting in the presence of the king of the criminal world. He hates gangsters. This is the man all other gangsters aspire to be.

Bobby needs the money from the Irish mob to help him go to college, to become an honest man who fights injustice. And he is sitting here, to request help in getting that money, from the very worst of the unjust.

To his horror, Bobby realizes he is sitting in Ricky Malone's presence to ask him for money which he ultimately hopes to use to destroy him – and it is too late to turn back.

*   *   *

If ever there were a time to keep on the mask, maintain his persona, it is now. It is absolutely imperative at this moment that he not let it be shown that he is far more afraid than young Bobby Falcone. He's been trying in vain to prepare for this moment. He keeps a glass of scotch on his desk to help ease his nerves, but it is not doing the trick. But no matter. Malone has had a lifetime of experience in hiding his fear, in appearing invincible.

When the boy walks through the door, Malone's heart stops beating for a few moments. Falcone has no idea that Malone has known who he is since the day he was born.

He is beautiful.

Tall, black hair, olive skin. But what really gets Malone are Falcone's eyes. Big, deep brown eyes, with very long eyelashes. He has Maria's eyes.

He is afraid he will not be able to conduct this meeting, but then he remembers – he is Ricky Malone. He's done this a million times.

*But not with Bobby.*

He knows what he has to do. He knows everything that is about to happen, and this is why he's so afraid.

But it is for the greater good of himself, of Bobby Falcone, and of the city.

He is truthfully amused by Falcone's sudden terrified reaction to the mention of his name, but also ashamed that the only connotation that the boy has to his name is negative.

*It is my own fault,* he thinks. *But I will fix it. I will fix everything.*

*   *   *

Never on a single occasion in his eighteen years of life has Bobby felt a terror such as this. Sitting in the presence of Ricky Malone, he feels that any wrong word, the slightest miscommunication could get his head blown clear off.

Malone gives a slight chuckle to Bobby's reaction to his name, then says, "Who'd you think you were meeting, kid, President Hoover?" He takes a puff of his cigar, and slowly pushes out a large cloud, filling the air even more with the scent of tobacco. He chuckles and says in a low voice, "He's actually a pal of mine. I helped get him into the White House. Good guy. Helped me fix the series a few years back."

Bobby cannot believe the things he is hearing. He is so immensely overwhelmed that he does not even know what to feel.

"But enough of that," he continues, taking a sip from his glass with the same hand whose index and middle fingers hold his cigar.

"What can I do for you today, Mr. Falcone?"

Bobby struggles to find the words, wondering if he should even ask. Why on earth would this man want to help him get his money back?

But he remembers, this is his one shot. On top of that, if Falcone came all this way, and wasted Malone's time and didn't even bother to ask his favor, Malone would be annoyed. And Ricky Malone is the last person you'd want to annoy.

Bobby opens his mouth, but no sound comes out; he moves his mouth but no words are formed.

"Some water, kid?" Malone says contemptuously.

"Uh, no," Bobby replies nervously. He must look so stupid right now.

"So, Mr. Malone," he begins, trying his best to conceal his terror.

"I had some money, in the bank. Five grand. I couldn't get to it until I was eighteen, and I was going to use it to go to college. So I go to take it out, and they tell me it's gone. I know it was Gallagher and his boys. The money was in their bank. Would've been real easy for them to snatch it up."

Malone is silent. Before he continues, it occurs to Bobby that he shouldn't tell Malone that he thought he would be meeting with a legitimate businessman.

"So uh, a friend of mine told me you might be willing to help me out. I'm more than willing to pay up. Out of the five grand, you could take five hundred. A thousand even, if you think that's more appropriate."

Bobby realizes that he's talking extremely fast. At this point, he's just happy he can speak without wetting his pants. He is more concerned with making it out of this office alive than he is with getting his money back.

After a few moments, Malone says, "So," and he leans in.

His face comes into the faint light of the lamp, and Bobby can see him more clearly. His face is thin, and the wrinkles and lines on his face reveal his age to Bobby. He is clean shaven, and his graying hair is slicked back, similar to the man Bobby'd met downstairs. Something about his face seems vaguely familiar, as though Bobby had come across him before. Or perhaps, he was someone Bobby had known a long time ago. But Bobby knows that he has never seen this man before. Coming across Ricky Malone would have been engraved permanently on Bobby's memory, as he knows this night will be.

"You want me to help get five thousand bucks out of Braden Gallagher and the Irish gang," he continues, his aged face twisting into a smile.

"Now why on God's green earth would I wanna go and do a thing like that?"

"Well, everyone knows you hate the Irish gang," Bobby says. He is utterly shocked that he was even able to think that fast, under all the pressure he is enduring right now. "I figured if anyone would want to get after them, it'd be you. I want money from them, you'd love to hurt them. And the enemy of my enemy is my friend, right? I'd like very much to be your friend."

Why did he say that? Why? Why on earth did Bobby tell Ricky Malone, probably the most dangerous man in the country, that he wanted to be his friend? The words had escaped his mouth before he even had time to think. It's as if someone else had said it for him. What did he just do?

*Oh, God.*

"Oh," Malone says, with a look of surprised amusement on his face. "Bobby Falcone would like to be my friend, huh?"

Malone stands up slowly and begins walking around the table. Bobby's heart pounds harder and faster with every step Malone takes toward him.

"What about this, Mr. Falcone? What if you're a cop, trying to set me up? This could be a whole little operation, leading me straight into a trap?" He chuckles a bit, then says, "Who am I kidding? If all the cops in this city aren't mine, most of them are. But even better, what if *you* are one of Gallagher's boys, under cover. What if you just wanna take me home to your boys, and blow me away?"

Bobby hears the click of a pistol cocking, and feels the cold metal against his temple.

"What would be keeping me from spilling your brains all over my floor right now?"

Bobby is absolutely petrified. He thought he was afraid before, but now, he actually half hopes Malone would pull the trigger, just to get Bobby out of this situation. Bobby has never even seen a gun before. Now, there is a cocked, loaded pistol pressed up against his head, in the hands of a seasoned killer who would release a bullet without so much as a second thought, and proceed to sleep like a baby the same night. His entire body is cold and his muscles are so tense he feels he will never move again. He wonders if he is even still alive, and desperately hopes that this isn't real, but that he has been plunged into one of his most horrid nightmares from which he will soon wake up.

"Well," Bobby musters up all the courage he can to say, with barely more than a whisper, "I suppose you'll just have to trust me. And if you don't," Bobby wonders if he has the audacity to actually utter the words he is about to. "Just shoot me now."

Malone laughs again. "Just shoot you now."

He places the gun on the desk with a thud.

"You got balls kid, I like you. Most people, they come in here and run out with their pants soiled before they even ask me their favors. But you," he wags his finger at Bobby. "You mean business. I'll help you get your money back. And you know what," Malone looks up, thinking for a moment, "I'll do it myself. And this favor'll be for free. After all, we're the best of friends now, right?" He flashes his devilish smile, which irks Bobby although he is elated that he will be getting his money.

"You ready?" he says.

Bobby has no idea what to say, what to think. "R-ready for what?"

Malone chuckles again, and plops back down into his chair. Without a word more to Bobby, he picks up his phone and begins rotating the dial.

After a few moments, he says, "Gallagher. Malone. I'd like to engage in a little business with you. You and your boys love that whiskey, don't you."

He waits for an answer.

"Of course I can. If you're interested, I got about five grand worth of the stuff."

He pauses again, then says, "Listen, if you don't want it, there's plenty of other folks who'd pay a lot more than 5K for the whis...Yeah, that's what I thought. Meet me tomorrow night. The old warehouse area right before the bridge. And you listen to me, you better be alone. I'm bringing you your juice by myself. I see so much as one Smitty or Seamus, they might end up with a head full of lead and you'll never do business in this city again. You and me... Alright. Tomorrow, ten p.m. Bring all the cash. Don't be late." Malone quickly hangs up the phone.

He looks up at Bobby and says, "Alright, kid. Looks like you'll get that fancy education after all. Only one string. You gotta come with me tomorrow to get the cash."

*No!* Bobby wants to shout, but he stops himself. One of the wealthiest, most powerful men in the country just agreed to help him get back the five thousand dollars stolen from him, and for free. He is in no position to refuse to ride with Malone to get his own money. It was the least Malone could've asked for. No matter how terrified he'd be to go make the transaction with Gallagher, it would be one more night, and he'd never have to be a part of this world again. Or would he? Bobby tries to push it as far back in his mind as he can, that Malone now considers the two of them friends.

"Ok," Bobby murmurs.

"Good. Meet me here at nine-thirty tomorrow. Not a minute later. *Capice?*"

Bobby nods his head.

"Alright then. Get outta here," Malone says, gesturing to the door with his gun.

Bobby jumps up out of his seat without so much as a "thank you", and leaves as fast as he can. He has never been more relieved to leave any place, ever. He feels guilty for having accepted Malone's help, but there's something about knowing your future has just been handed back to you on a silver platter that dulls the feeling of guilt and puts a sweaty, frightened smile on your face.

* * *

Ricky Malone, the most dangerous, the most feared, easily the most powerful man in the world's greatest city, has never been more relieved to be finished with a meeting. He's never experienced fear of another human being until this day. No other man has ever made Malone feel small, made him feel inadequate, made him experience regret. Malone is proud of himself for remaining calm and collected during his meeting with Bobby Falcone.

However, the meeting also made Malone happy, in a strange, new way. In a way, meeting the boy warmed Malone's old, cold heart.

He refills the glass of scotch he had drunk clean, and takes a small sip. The burn in his throat makes him feel warm.

The boy was smart. He made Malone laugh. Malone felt proud of the eighteen-year-old boy he had just met for the very first time, though he also felt regret for the fact that that was their first meeting.

Malone picks up his pistol, feeling the cold metal in his hand. He enjoyed testing Falcone with it. Point a pistol at someone's head, and you find out what they're really made of. Malone was happy to see what Falcone was all about – he wasn't a coward. The kid had guts.

Malone pushes the empty cylinder out, and spins it around a few times. This gun has not been loaded in weeks.

*I'd never point a loaded gun at Bobby.*

But why, oh why, did he change the plan?

This was a first for Ricky Malone, a man who hasn't had a first of anything in decades. Had meeting Falcone shaken him up that much? Why did he call Gallagher? Why did he ask him about a transaction?

He knows good and well that he doesn't have five thousand dollars worth of whiskey, and for him to accumulate that much would take at least two or three weeks. Why had he told Gallagher to meet him tomorrow? And most importantly, *why in God's name had he told Bobby to come with him to get the money?*

Ricky Malone has never changed a plan once it had been set. *Especially* when he had no Plan B in order. The original plan was to show up at Gallagher's door, unannounced, with a few good men, squeeze every cent out of him, and then assassinate him, leaving no trace that he'd ever been on scene. He would give Bobby his money, then he'd disappear. Without a word, he'd abandon his empire. He'd flee the city, he'd find a way to start a life over, someplace that no one knew him. Maybe he even would have gone home to Naples and resided there permanently. And never, under any circumstances, would he tell Bobby how he knew him, why he was so eager to get him his money back.

But now what?

What on earth will he do tomorrow, when Bobby shows up, eager to get his money back? What on earth will he give Gallagher? How on earth will he manage to get five grand out of him? What on earth would happen?

Why, why, why had he abandoned his plan?

*Oh well. Everything will fall together.*

He downs the rest of the glass of scotch in one gulp, takes a long puff from his cigar, leans back in his chair and closes his eyes.

*I hope.*

*       *       *

Bobby pulls up to the office buildings in his cab. It is 9:27. He was afraid of being late, but sees that this will not be an issue. He pays the driver without a word, and steps out of the vehicle.

He didn't sleep a wink last night, and all day his full attention was fixated on what was about to happen. He skipped work, because he had not even enough calm to focus on sweeping up cut hair. He wandered the streets for hours, searching for Scraps. He has been furious with Scraps since the moment he heard the words "Ricky Malone." He planned on verbally berating him, if he had the discipline to resist beating the bum to a pulp.

He is not as blatantly terrified as he had been yesterday, though he is still very frightened. He knows what is going to happen today, and the certainty of the events about to unfold set his mind at ease. He is also content that today is the day that he will get back what was stolen from him. Do not misunderstand. He is very uneasy. There is no way to remain calm while walking toward the most dangerous criminal of the time, even if you have just met and become acquainted with him the previous day.

But after tonight, it will all be over.

He walks toward building 72 with haste. He passes the buildings preceding it, hardly looking up from the ground. The dead silence does not perturb Bobby as it had last night.

"Ready, kid?"

Bobby is startled. He expected to have to walk into the building once again. But he is surprised to see Ricky Malone outside, wearing a suit and tie, with a long black overcoat. A black fedora sits atop his head, casting a shadow over his eyes. A lit cigar hangs from his mouth, slowly releasing smoke into the night air. He is leaned back on a 1926 Rolls Royce Phantom, a giant black chariot for the dark king of New York.

The automobile probably costs more than Bobby's entire life leading up to this night.

Bobby pauses for a moment after hearing Malone's voice, then timidly nods his head.

Malone nods sharply once, chucks his cigar to the side of the road, and briskly walks to the driver's side door. Although Malone had said so on the phone, Bobby is very surprised to see that he would be driving them himself.

Bobby cautiously proceeds to the car, his fear growing once more. He didn't think about the time he would have to spend in the car alone with Malone. He opens the door very slowly, and sits down. He is very careful not to slam the door.

The interior of Malone's car reeks of tobacco and alcohol. All of the upholstery is solid red, like blood.

Malone turns the key in the ignition, and the car roars to a start. He pulls out of the parking space, and the journey begins.

As they drive, several heads on the road turn sharply to gaze at the car in which the two men ride. Bobby is sure that everyone who steals a glance knows the identity of the only person in the city wealthy enough to own a vehicle such as this one. Bobby is uncomfortable with being seen with Ricky Malone, but then notices the windows of the car are tinted. He also remembers – everyone in New York is far too afraid of Malone to report seeing anything that has to do with him.

After what seems like ages of riding through Brooklyn, they arrive at the venue at which they will make their transaction. It's an old warehouse district right before the Brooklyn Bridge. It is clear to Bobby that Malone only conducts his affairs in abandoned areas where there will be no witnesses. Not that the prospect of witnesses is threatening to him, it is probably simply more "professional."

There is an open gate between two buildings leading into the small district, with a passage wide enough for only one car to fit through at a time. Inside the gate is an open area – a courtyard between several of the warehouses.

They pull to the right of the courtyard, and Malone parks the car and removes his key. On the opposite side of the courtyard is parked another car, a white Mercedes-Benz.

"There he is," Malone says in a low voice, gesturing to the car.

Right after he says this, the driver across the way steps out of his car, clutching a briefcase. He walks to the passenger side of the car, stands still, and stares across at the Phantom, holding the briefcase by the handle with both hands in front of his body.

Gallagher is huge. He must be close to three hundred pounds, about six-foot-three. The top of his head is bald, and he has graying red hair circling his head. His cheeks hang below his severe frown like a bulldog, and his eyes are black and dead, like a great white shark. He is dressed in a buttoned, black shirt, encompassed by a white suit jacket. His pants and shoes are also snow-white. He is absolutely terrifying. However, in some strange way, Malone still sends colder chills running up Bobby's spine.

"Show time," Malone says to Bobby, with a smile that greatly disturbs him.

What on earth does he mean, show time? Why had he smiled as though he had some secret devious plan? These questions would go unanswered, as Malone opens the car door and steps out. He goes to the back of his car and removes a large, closed crate. Bobby hears the clank of glass inside as Malone walks toward Gallagher. The crate looks almost too large for Malone's thin frame to handle, but he manages. Bobby's heart begins to practice its six-punch combination on the interior of his ribcage once more. He was relatively calm up until this moment, but that is over with. Once again, Bobby wishes he were anyone but himself, anywhere but here.

It was just a quick business deal, right? A quick trade, the money for the whiskey? Why had Malone seemed so devilishly excited to leave the car? What was going to happen when he reached Gallagher and spoke to him?

Malone is about three-quarters of the way across.

*Well, whatever is going to happen is going to happen right now.*

*   *   *

There is a certain thrill in bluffing. There's a certain excitement in allowing your opponents to believe you have the flush, when all you actually have is a few low numerals, maybe one face card. However, this excitement also comes with nerves, and fear, because if someone calls your bluff, all will be lost. It is nerve-wracking enough when the stakes are chips, maybe a few thousand dollars, but in Malone's case, it could be life or death. This is the reason behind the quiet dread he feels, walking toward Braden Gallagher and his five grand with a crate full of empty bottles.

He feels he could have come up with a better plan, but for some reason, he doesn't seem to care. He is oddly content with the choice he made. After all, it is *Malone's* city. What would Gallagher really dare to do? At least, that is the notion that Malone is running with.

He was so fixated on this transaction throughout the day that he hadn't even been shaken up by the ride with Bobby, as he would have been yesterday.

His heart pounds harder with every step he takes toward the huge Irish figure before him. However, none of his terror would be shown on the outside. He is sure of that. In bluffing out your opponent, your most important weapon is your poker face – and as far as weapons go, Malone's poker face is a ship-sinking torpedo.

*It'll all be over soon.*

Malone stops about five feet in front of Gallagher. The two gangsters are silent for a moment, until Gallagher says, "Do you have my whiskey?" His Irish accent is thick and affects every syllable he speaks.

"Do you have my money?" Malone replies immediately.

Gallagher looks down, gesturing with his eyes toward the briefcase he holds.

"First give me the whiskey."

Malone is silent for half a moment.

"Do you know where you are standing?" he says, placing the crate on the ground. "You are standing in *my* city. This whiskey, it's *my* whiskey. That five grand you're holding, it's *my* money. This warehouse district belongs to me. Your territory is my backyard. I'm papa bear. I'm the boss. Nothing goes on here without my okay. I coulda walked up to you and your boys and beaten the money out of you, without so much as a moment's hesitation, without you having a chance of slowing me down, and the cops would have nothing to say about it. But out of the kindness of an old man's heart, I decided to give you a little something for it. So don't you allow yourself even for a hot second to become so comfortable in my town that you think you can tell me what to do, *capice?*"

The two are silent once again. Gallagher does not know what to say.

"Drop the cash," Malone says.

Gallagher hastily drops the briefcase to the ground, and slides it to Malone with his foot. Malone smiles.

"You have your money. Now give me my whiskey!" he says.

"Alright, bub, hold your horses." Malone copies Gallagher in placing his crate onto the ground, then heaving it to Gallagher's feet. It nudges his foot, and he bends down to open it. Malone's heart is racing, and a drop of sweat runs down his forehead. But he is ready.

Gallagher gets the top of the crate open after trying for a few moments, and he withdraws a bottle. Immediately upon seeing it is empty, he says "Huh?" His face twists into a hideous scowl, and he looks sharply up at Malone.

In one smooth, swift motion, Malone strips the holster underneath his overcoat of its shiny silver pistol, cocks it, and points it directly at Gallagher's face.

"You're gonna close that bank, get outta New York, and never steal from any innocent boy again, you hear me?"

A swift "yes, sir" is the answer Malone is accustomed to. Gallagher, however, has other intentions. He drops the bottle to the ground, shattering it, and reaches under his jacket while muttering "You dirty Italian."

Malone knows exactly what that means. He hadn't quite planned for this.

He immediately picks up the briefcase and begins sprinting back to his car, firing backwards.

*Bang, Bang, BANG!*

He assumes that Gallagher ran behind his car for cover, but then hears gunshots that are not his, and feels bullets whizzing inches past him.

He looks back for a brief second, and lets two more bullets fly. One of them blows Gallagher's kneecap. Gallagher gives a huge, pained shriek and falls to the ground. Now Malone just has to get back to Bobby in his car, and speed out of there. Why is the car so far? Malone feels as though he had walked fifty feet to Gallagher and is running a mile back. Malone has not been this terrified, this exhilarated, this excited, this scared for his life, since long before he claimed the throne of the Big Apple. After running what feels like a marathon, he reaches his car. He drops the briefcase to grab the handle of the door.

*Bang!*

Malone is on the ground, clutching his side, the meat just above his left hip. The bullet lodges itself in the metal of the Phantom after making its way cleanly through Malone's flesh. He feels as though he had just been walloped in front and in back by a heavyweight boxer, then the wound set on fire. He knows it is just a flesh wound, but begins to panic anyway. Throughout his entire career in his precarious business, Malone has never been shot. His heart races even faster than it had before, and he begins hyperventilating. He severely aggravates the pain in his side by clutching it with all his strength to stop the bleeding.

However, even while running in a blind panic, Malone had been counting, and knows that that was Gallagher's last bullet.

He looks back and fires, but Gallagher is already inside his car, a small puddle of blood on the ground where he had been. Malone's shot shatters the driver's side window, but does not hit Gallagher.

That was Malone's last shot, as well.

*I have another gun in the glove box.*

Malone pushes the briefcase underneath the car to the other side, and, summoning all of his strength, throws himself over the hood of his car. The pain of doing this feels like getting shot again, but Malone knows it is far better to have felt this pain than to remain in Gallagher's line of fire. No doubt Gallagher, too, has another gun.

Malone plops to the ground, not strong enough to land on his feet. His entire body slams into the ground with a thud, and Malone groans. Looking down, he sees that his hand is covered in blood, and there is a very large red stain on his white shirt around his wound.

"This was my favorite shirt," Malone says to himself through gritted teeth.

The passenger door bursts open, and Bobby falls out. He has thrown himself out to get behind the car for more cover as well. His face is drenched in sweat and tears, and his eyes bloodshot.

"Ricky, what is happening! Why did you shootwhyisheshootingwhydidntyoujustgivehimthevod-"

Bobby's hysteria is cut off by the sound of Gallagher's engine. Malone and Falcone hear tires skidding, the car moving a very short distance very quickly. Malone peers under the car to get a better view, and his heart stops. Gallagher has moved his car to the spot directly in front of the opening of the courtyard, blocking them all in.

"Malone, you scum!" they hear him shout.

"You've got to get up sometime! I will wait for you all night!"

Malone looks from Bobby, who is a mess, to his own bloodstained side, back up to Gallagher, who is slowly trying to stand up out of his car on one leg, another gun drawn. There is no way out.

*What have I done?*

*       *       *

Bobby's heart is beating so fast he is beginning to wonder if it is even a heart at all. Maybe it's a hummingbird that had gotten lost and ducked for cover in his chest. Maybe it's even a locomotive engine that the manufacturer had used to power Bobby instead of their trains. Or maybe it's Whiskers, the rabbit that ran away when Bobby was eleven, thumping with his huge feet on Bobby's ribs.

Bobby thought he was scared in the seventh grade when Jimmy De Luca had beaten him up for his lunch money. He even thought he was scared when he found out the businessman was Ricky Malone. He even, for a brief moment, believed he was feeling fear when he got into

Malone's Phantom to meet up with Gallagher. But now, scared isn't even the correct word.

Bobby Falcone is absolutely terrified. What he feels now is the most basic, instinctual, deepest, and truest fear any living creature can experience – fear for his life. For the first time in eighteen years, Bobby is seriously questioning whether or not he will survive the night.

It had made him uncomfortable the way Ricky smiled when he got out of his car. It had made him slightly more uncomfortable to see how long Malone and Gallagher were talking before anything happened. But when Malone drew his gun, Bobby immediately knew that he was in danger. It was supposed to be a simple deal: money for whiskey, tit for tat. He could not, for the life of him, understand why Malone had drawn a gun. Just as Bobby began losing it, thinking hard about the fact that until yesterday he'd never even seen a gun, he heard breathtakingly loud gunshots breaking through the night air.

His hands had flown to his ears without so much as a thought, and he shouted Ricky's name over and over. It seemed he took forever to reach the car. He saw Gallagher's leg get taken out from under him, and thought briefly that he and Ricky were safe. But then, from the ground, Gallagher let another shot go, and Malone went down. Gallagher crawled up into his car, but Malone was nowhere to be seen.

His whole life, Bobby has viewed himself as a good person, an honest person who would become a legitimate professional – certainly not the type of person to be in the company of gangsters, to be shielding his ears from the sound of gunshots. It's funny how fast everything can change.

*Being shot? That would never, ever happen to me.*

But it happened to Ricky Malone, the most powerful man in New York City, probably the country, right before his eyes. Bobby saw the blood spatter on the window, heard Malone's pained grunt, heard the thud of Malone's body as it hit the ground. The bullet didn't care who Malone was. If a bullet didn't stop for Ricky Malone, why on earth would it stop for Bobby Falcone?

*Bang!*

Gallagher's window shatters, and before he knows it, Ricky Malone is flying over the hood of the car, leaving a thin trail of blood on the hood where he slid.

*Gallagher will keep shooting to try and kill him,* Bobby thinks. He knows he's not safe in the passenger seat, directly in view of the windows.

In an instant, he opens his door and throws himself out, landing right next to Malone. He is livid with Malone. He has never been so thoroughly enraged at another human being in his entire life. His blood pressure is comparable to the water pressure of a fire hose. Malone is already shot, and now Bobby's own life is on the line. He doesn't even know where to begin, but he voices his grievances the best he can, just letting out a long stream of angered questions.

But before he knows what's happening, he hears Gallagher driving. He looks away from Malone, and under the car to see what Gallagher is doing.

*Maybe he's fleeing. Maybe we can still get out.*

No.

Exactly the opposite is happening. Gallagher's car is parked in front of the only way out, and he's yelling to Malone that he will wait there all night for him. He will wait all night to kill him, and then, no doubt, Bobby.

They are trapped.

"Ricky, RICKY! What are we going to do?!"

"Oh, alone, are you, Malone?" Gallagher yells. "I should have known you would never travel alone!"

*Crap.*

Bobby had just given it away that he was with Malone. He forgot that Gallagher thought Malone was by himself. Any chance of getting away if Malone is killed is down the drain.

"Move!" Malone says in a low voice. Still fiercely clutching his bullet wound, he reaches up into his car and opens his glove box.

*Bang! Bang! Bang!*

Bullets are ricocheting off of Malone's car.

*Bang!*

One breaks through the windshield.

*Bang!*

Another whizzes right past Bobby. He can feel the wind.

"Ricky! He's going to kill us!"

Bobby is hysterical. He no longer cares that Gallagher can hear him. He doesn't care how he sounds to Gallagher or to Malone. He's only eighteen. He's barely begun to live. He didn't even tell his mother he was leaving the house.

Malone pulls another pistol out of his glove box, cocks it, and begins firing in Gallagher's direction. At the sound of his shots, Gallagher stops shooting. Bobby figures he is ducking for cover.

"Ricky, what are we gonna-"

Ricky begins to chuckle a weak, pained laugh. He is still clutching his wound, and breathing very heavily.

"Get out here. Malone! Face me like a man!" The two hear Gallagher shout.

"My boy," Malone says, laying his palm on Bobby's face.

"Ricky, what are you doing?" Bobby says, utterly confused.

"My boy," he says again, still panting.

"Show yourself, Malone!" Gallagher barks.

"I remember when you were born," Ricky pants.

"Ricky what the he-"

"Your mother. She knew what kind of man I was. She wanted nothing to do with me."

"My mother? Ricky, come on, you're talking crazy. We gotta get out of-"

"I told her. I says, 'You're not keeping my son away from me.' But she didn't want her son raised with a father like me."

Bobby is absolutely silent. He feels like his ears are bleeding, and his head is about to fall off. His heart, which was just beating so rapidly, has closed up shop for the night. What Malone is implying cannot possibly be true.

"But then you were born. You were so small, so beautiful," Malone says, still smiling, though a single tear runs down his cheek. "I knew that I couldn't raise you. I couldn't make you a part of the world I was a part of. So your mother and I agreed. You wouldn't know me, you wouldn't know who I was."

Bobby cannot bear to hear any more of this. "Shut your mouth," he says to Malone. "You shut your mouth!"

"Malone, you coward! Show yourself!" Gallagher sounds rabid, and another bullet finds its way over the Phantom.

"So I left you five grand. I left you a little piece of me. I know five grand is no father, but it's the most I could do."

"You keep me and my mother out of your mouth, you hear me?" Bobby shouts, tears filling his eyes once more, his voice shaking.

"When it was stolen, I had to get it back. I had to get it-" It seems Ricky can no longer speak. He has no voice. More tears fall from his eyes.

"I'm so sorry, Bobby. I'm so sorry."

Bobby covers his face in his hands. He cannot handle any more of this.

*I suppose I was right. I had a rich father who left the money for me.*

This man, the shadow of New York, the king, the absolute worst gangster there is, is Bobby's father. He has no more room in his heart for fear. At this moment, he does not even care if a bullet hits him and strikes him dead. He is not scared, he is not sad, he is not happy, he is not angry. And at the same time, he is all of those things. All his life, the father he'd missed had been right in front of his eyes, watching over him, but Bobby would never have wanted to see him. How is anyone supposed to feel about that? And his mother, she had a hand in keeping his father away from him. How can he ever look her in the eyes again, knowing she had helped rob him of a father? And yet, how could he be angry at either of them? His father was a vicious criminal, the very type of person Bobby wanted nothing to do with, who he wanted to destroy. Both of his parents had helped keep him away from this man, this dark, powerful, wonderful man. His father, Ricky Malone.

"I will make this right, Bobby. I'll make this all right. Stay here. I'll finish this."

Ricky grabs the car door, and begins pulling himself up.

"No, Ricky, wait," Bobby says through his tears. "He'll kill you." His whole life, Bobby has never known whether he wanted to hug his father or punch him in the mouth, but right now, he knows that he just doesn't want him to leave his side. For the desire to be close to a father, for fear for his life. He grabs onto Ricky's coat, but he brushes his hand off.

"Take this," Ricky says, removing a large ring from his left pinky. "My father gave it to me, and his before him. It's only right…" He places the ring in Bobby's hand.

Ricky continues getting up.

"Ricky, I can't…" Bobby stares at the ring in his hand. He cannot cope with everything that is happening right now. How much is this ring worth? How far had it come? Bobby closes his fingers around the ring, and finds it increasingly difficult to breathe.

"No one's laying a finger on my boy. Not tonight."

Ricky lets go of his side, and takes his pistol in both hands as he stands up. "When it's safe, run. Take the money, run as fast as you can, and don't look back. Don't ever look back. Go to Harvard, come back, be better than I ever could be. You'll be a great man some day, kid. I know it." Malone looks away, turns his head far to one side to crack his neck, and readjusts the fedora on his head.

"Let's see how good a shot your old man is, uh?"

*   *   *

The home stretch. For the first time in what feels like a very, very long time, Ricky Malone feels at peace. You may ask what kind of man feels at peace in the middle of a shootout, about to face an Irish gangster whose greatest wish is to kill him, a crying son on the ground behind him, and intending to shoot a man. No ordinary man should be at ease in this moment.

But Ricky Malone is no ordinary man.

At the present, he is at peace.

His boy knows who he is. His son has met him for the first time. His son knows that he has a father. His son has the money he left him. His son is safe – well, he's still working on that.

A sixty-year-old man with a bullet wound in his side should have had a much harder time standing up, but Malone does it with ease. Nothing is ever that hard when you have help. The dark, evil shadow of New York City, the one who is known as a thief, a merciless killer, the man who once taunted him in the mirror, helps Malone up on his left. The good man underneath that no one knew but him, the man who once refused to think of letting his son grow up without a father, the one who left his son a gift of five thousand dollars to make a life with, and who ultimately made the decision to keep his innocent boy away from a life of crime and murder, helps Malone up on his right.

He is on his feet, ready to face Gallagher.

Malone does not know why he abandoned his original plan, why he duped Gallagher, or why he told Bobby to accompany him. Then again, he also does not know why he chose a life of crime, why he ever picked up a pistol, why he was so power-hungry and driven by the idea of fortune and prestige in his youth. Perhaps he will never know.

Perhaps he truly is just a crazy old man, acting increasingly foolishly as he slowly loses his mind. Perhaps the weight of guilt of decades of crime has finally crushed his soul, leaving him helpless, not knowing what to do. Perhaps he knows that the end is near, that his final curtain call is approaching, and needs for Bobby to know who he is, even if that means risking his life for his son's. Perhaps he is so hell-bent on getting his son's money back that he is acting foolishly, recklessly, like a cornered animal. Perhaps the hand of fate has been marking his path the entire way. Perhaps, deep down, Ricky Malone truly does have a death wish.

Malone stands up straight and takes several quick steps forward, trying to distance himself from Bobby. Gallagher's gun is directed straight at Malone's chest. Malone looks directly into Gallagher's cold, black, murderous eyes, but he feels no fear. Ricky Malone fears no man.

There is one bullet in Malone's gun. Gallagher has three.

Malone holds his pistol up. Staring down the shaft of his gun, he can see the sweet spot on Gallagher's forehead, just between his eyes. Malone knows that when his eyes are set on a target, he does not miss.

*Bang!* Malone's bullet is released.

*Bang! Bang! Bang!* All of Gallagher's bullets fly.

Three bullets fly east, one flies west.

Every bullet strikes true.

Bobby is safe.

All of Malone's struggles have come to a close. His worries are no more.

*     *     *

It is a warm fall day in Cambridge, Massachusetts. As Bobby looks out of his dormitory room window, he reflects on everything that had to happen in order for him to get here.

He has come to grips with the fact that his father was Ricky Malone, the most feared man in the country. He had several very bitter arguments with his mother, but they eventually reconciled the issue.

Bobby has thought about that night every moment of every passing day, for the last three and a half months. The night he was witness to two murders. The night he had met his father for the first time, then had him stripped from his life once more. The night he picked up a briefcase full of money, tried to look away from the two dead gangsters on the ground before him, and fled through the night as fast as he possibly could away from the horrible scene, never glancing back.

That night changed Bobby's life forever. For better or worse, that was left to Bobby to decide.

He always wanted to go to Harvard, become a lawyer, eventually a politician, and return home to New York to make a lasting positive impact on the lives of people just like himself.

What does it say about Bobby that the very worst of all the street scum, the very man Bobby once hoped to destroy, had paid for Bobby to gain that education? What does it say that Ricky Malone, of all people, believed in Bobby's cause?

Bobby knows he has a grave responsibility to use Ricky's money for what it was meant for, to milk Harvard University for all it could offer him, and to become the man that both he and his father knew he could be.

He will never know all the details, but Bobby does know this: he was not a model citizen, perhaps he was not even a good man at all, but his father did care about him. The father who once tried to buy his son's admiration with five thousand dollars, had paid for it with his life.

Bobby knows, beyond reasonable doubt, that without Ricky Malone, he would never, in a million years, be sitting in a dorm at Harvard University. That is worth something.

"Hey, Bobby, come on, we're gonna be late," his friend calls behind him.

"I'm coming," Bobby answers.

Bobby looks down at the ring on his left pinky. He twirls it around his finger once, then draws his hand to his mouth and kisses it.

He turns quickly around and leaves his room, closing the door behind him. No matter what has happened to him in the past, what was given, what was taken, Bobby Falcone has emerged all the better for it. Today belongs to him.

# About the Author

Tyler Brooks, a native of Paterson, New Jersey, is a lover of literature and an avid reader and writer. He is eighteen years old and is currently a freshman at American University, majoring in literature with a concentration in cinema.

45492479R00035